# Respecting Your Mother

DISCARD

Published by Ali Gator Productions
Copyright © 2018 Ali Gator Productions, Second Edition,
First Published 2016

National Library of Australia Cataloguing–in-Publication (CIP) data:
Dian A. Dewi, Respecting Your Mother
ISBN: 978-1-921772-35-1
For primary school age, Juvenile fiction, Dewey Number: 823.92

Adapted from the original title Senangnya Membantu Ibu first published by Dar! Mizan.
Copyright© 2009 by Author Dian A. Dewi, Illustrator Studio Air. Printed in Indonesia.

T: +61 (3) 9386 2771 F: +61 (3) 9478 8854
P.O. Box 2536, Regent West, Melbourne Victoria, 3072 Australia
E: info@ali-gator.com W: www.ali-gator.com

■ ■ ■ ■ ■

The aim of the Akhlaaq Building for Kids Series is to inspire young children to develop good Akhlaaq (manners) through fun stories involving young children like themselves.

The main characters are a young girl Saaliha and her younger brother Ali.

Along with their friends they experience various situations, all with a moral message for the young readers.

In Sha Allah (God Willing) if this series helps to inspire our young readers to be better people, following the best of example in manners and behavior, the Prophet Muhammad (peace be upon him), then we have truly achieved our goal.

*BISMILLAHIR RAHMANIR RAHIM*
IN THE NAME OF ALLAH, MOST GRACIOUS, MOST MERCIFUL

Saaliha and Ali were playing together
when they heard their mother come home.
They were both so happy
to hear her car outside the house.

"Let's go and help Mama," said an excited Saaliha.

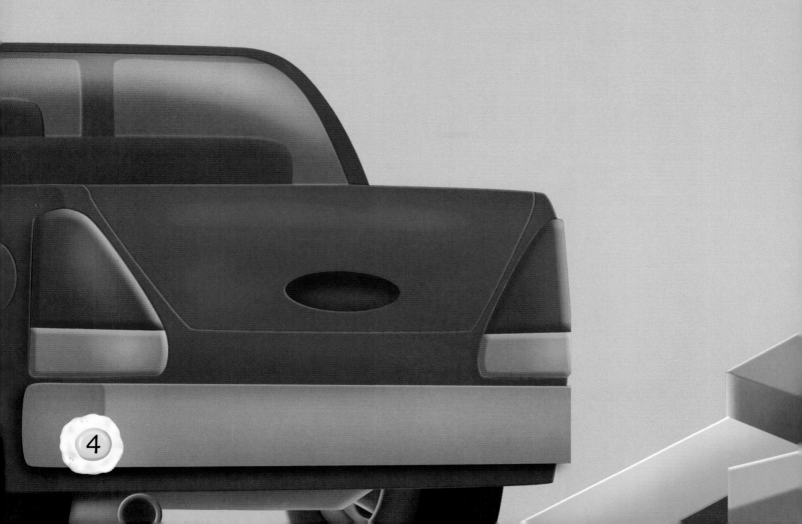

4

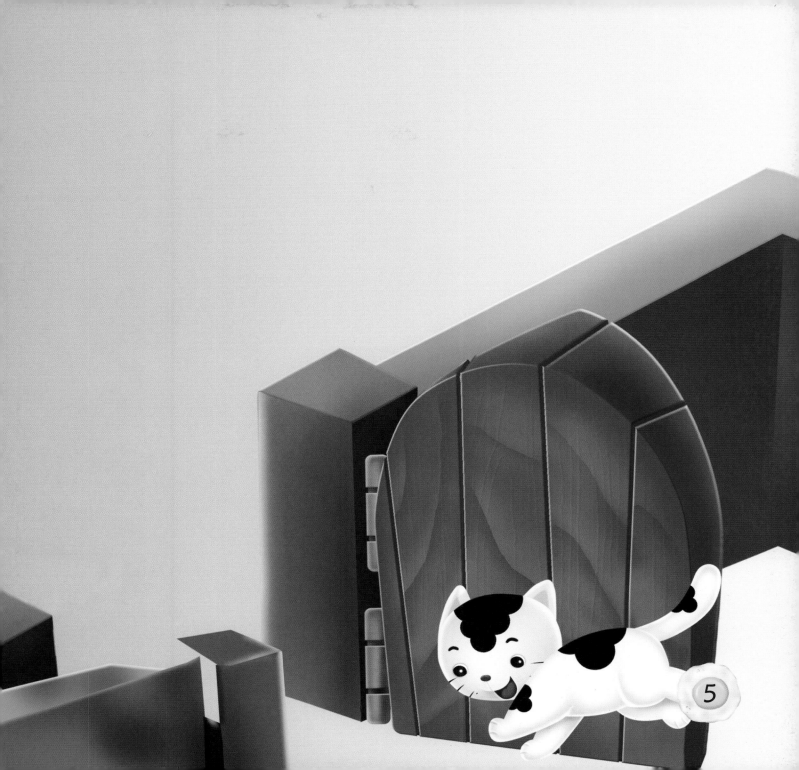

Their mother had been shopping and had many bags to carry.

"Mama, Ma Sha Allah you have a lot of things, let me help you bring them inside," said a surprised Ali.

*MA SHA ALLAH - ALLAH HAS WILLED IT*

"Can I carry the vegetables?" asked Saaliha.

"Thank you darling,
you're always willing to help me out,
you're such a good girl,"
answered their mother.

"What about me, can I carry something ?" asked an excited Ali.

"Of course you can," replied his grateful mother.

"You can carry my other bag, you're a good helping boy too," said his mother smiling.

Even Mia the cat helped out carrying a bag. Nobody wanted to miss out helping Saaliha and Ali's mother.

It was now easier for their mother to carry the rest of the shopping into the house.

13

Saaliha and Ali also like to help their mother by packing away the shopping.

Ali carefully packs the eggs away, whilst Saaliha helps her mother by washing the tomatoes.

15

Both Saaliha and Ali know the rewards for respecting and helping their mother.

Saaliha even helps their mother with the cooking.

Ali is still a bit young to help with many things, even if he thinks he's a big boy.

But Ali can do other things around the house to help. He feeds their pet cat Mia and cleans the cat's bowl.

Ali also helps clear the table after they eat dinner together as a family.

Saaliha learnt a Hadith at the mosque, which says.

"Jannah lies under the feet of your mother"*

To earn Allah's pleasure both Saaliha and Ali love and respect their mother and help her whenever they can.

So be good to your mother and father and Allah will be pleased with you too, and grant you the greatest reward, Jannah, In Sha Allah.

* as recorded by
  [Musnad Ahmad, Sunan
  An-Nasâ'i, Sunan Ibn Mâjah]

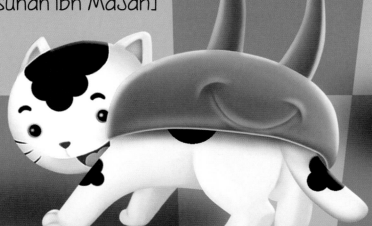

JANNAH - HEAVEN
IN SHA ALLAH - GOD WILLING

21

Saaliha and Ali's mother loves how
they both help her around the house.

She loves both of them more and more every day.

*ALHAMDULILLAH*
PRAISE BE TO ALLAH